Dear Parent:

Congratulations! Your child is taking the first steps on an exciting journey. The destination? Independent reading!

STEP INTO READING® will help your child get there. The program offers five steps to reading success. Each step includes fun stories and colorful art. There are also Step into Reading Sticker Books, Step into Reading Math Readers, Step into Reading Phonics Readers, Step into Reading Write-In Readers, and Step into Reading Phonics Boxed Sets—a complete literacy program with something to interest every child.

Learning to Read, Step by Step!

Ready to Read   Preschool–Kindergarten
• big type and easy words • rhyme and rhythm • picture clues
For children who know the alphabet and are eager to begin reading.

Reading with Help   Preschool–Grade 1
• basic vocabulary • short sentences • simple stories
For children who recognize familiar words and sound out new words with help.

Reading on Your Own   Grades 1–3
• engaging characters • easy-to-follow plots • popular topics
For children who are ready to read on their own.

Reading Paragraphs   Grades 2–3
• challenging vocabulary • short paragraphs • exciting stories
For newly independent readers who read simple sentences with confidence.

Ready for Chapters   Grades 2–4
• chapters • longer paragraphs • full-color art
For children who want to take the plunge into chapter books but still like colorful pictures.

STEP INTO READING® is designed to give every child a successful reading experience. The grade levels are only guides. Children can progress through the steps at their own speed, developing confidence in their reading, no matter what their grade.

Remember, a lifetime love of reading starts with a single step!

For Lorie Ann Grover
—J.H.

To all the budding ballerinas everywhere
—S.M.

Published in the United States by Random House Children's Books, a division of Random House, Inc., 1745 Broadway, New York, NY 10019.

Step into Reading, Random House, and the Random House colophon are registered trademarks of Random House, Inc.

Visit us on the Web!
StepIntoReading.com
randomhouse.com/kids

Educators and librarians, for a variety of teaching tools, visit us at
randomhouse.com/teachers

Library of Congress Cataloging-in-Publication Data
Holub, Joan.
Ballet stars / by Joan Holub ; illustrated by Shelagh McNicholas. — 1st ed.
    p.   cm. — (Step into reading. A step 1 book)
Summary: Two friends get ready and then dance with their ballet class at a performance where they are the stars of the show.
ISBN 978-0-375-86909-9 (trade) — ISBN 978-0-375-96909-6 (lib. bdg.)
[1. Stories in rhyme. 2. Ballet dancing—Fiction.] I. McNicholas, Shelagh, ill. II. Title.
PZ8.3.H74Bal 2012
[E]—dc23   2011032047

Printed in the United States of America
10 9 8 7 6 5 4 3 2 1

STEP INTO READING®

Ballet Stars

by Joan Holub
illustrated by Shelagh McNicholas

Random House 🏠 New York

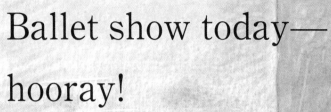

Ballet show today—
hooray!

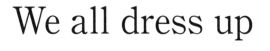

We all dress up
a fancy way.

Sparkly ribbons.

Ballet shoes.

Bright white tights.

And new tutus.

We do stretches.
We do bends.

We warm up
with ballet friends.

Ballet arms.

Ballet feet.

Toes point out

and fingers meet.

Here we go
across the floor.

We run three steps,
then jump on <u>four.</u>

Look who's come to see our show!

Our families and
some friends we know.

The music starts.

We find our places.

Happy smiles
on all our faces.

Twirl like snowflakes.

Sway like trees.

Dancing steps
in twos and threes.

Ballet dancers
in two rows
do ballet turns
on tippy-toes.

We bow to the left.

Blow kisses right.

We are ballet stars
tonight!